10632794

WHY YOU'L
by Lyn

Witches need black cats, and Theo and Dodie have one. Good luck – or bad?

When Mrs Scarum the witch blows in, scariness comes too, and the story of her doings on the night of the great blizzard that threatens Theo and Dodie's dad, kept me reading until way past the witching hour.

Full of adventure and spooky atmosphere. I loved it.

Lynne Reid Banks

Lynne Reid Banks was born in London in 1929. She was an actress in the late 1940s and early 1950s and later became one of the first two women TV News reporters in Britain. She is a best-selling author for both children and adults, and has written over forty books, including *The Indian in the Cupboard*, *I, Houdini* and *Harry the Poisonous Centipede*.

For Becky

First published in Great Britain by Collins Children's Books in 1996
This edition published by HarperCollins*Children'sBooks* in 2010
Collins is an imprint of HarperCollins*Publishers* Ltd.
HarperCollins*Children'sBooks* is a division of HarperCollins*Publishers* Ltd,
77-85 Fulham Palace Road, Hammersmith, London W6 8JB

The HarperCollins website address is
www.harpercollins.co.uk

1

Text copyright © Jenny Nimmo 1996
Illustrations by Thierry Elfezzani
Why You'll Love This Book copyright © Lynne Reid Banks 2010

ISBN-13 978 0 00 736471 8

Printed and bound in England by Clays Ltd, St Ives plc

Conditions of Sale
This book is sold subject to the condition
that it shall not, by way of trade or otherwise,
be lent, re-sold, hired out or otherwise circulated
without the publisher's prior consent in any form,
binding or cover other than that in which it is
published and without a similar condition
including this condition being imposed on the
subsequent purchaser.

Mixed Sources
Product group from well-managed
forests and other controlled sources
www.fsc.org Cert no. SW-COC-001806
© 1996 Forest Stewardship Council
FSC

FSC is a non-profit international organisation established to promote the
responsible management of the world's forests. Products carrying the FSC
label are independently certified to assure consumers that they come
from forests that are managed to meet the social, economic and
ecological needs of present and future generations.

Find out more about HarperCollins and the environment at
www.harpercollins.co.uk/green

The
Witch's
Tears

Jenny Nimmo

Illustrated by Thierry Elfezzani

HarperCollins *Children's Books*

Chapter One

It was an icy day. The wind was cold enough to freeze your breath and dark clouds tore across the sky like ragged horses.

Theo, running home from school, wished that his house was closer. It stood right at the end of the village street, a small stone cottage with a dark wood behind it. They called it The Clock House, because Theo's father collected and mended clocks: old clocks with chipped feet and scratched faces that nobody wanted; clocks with pendulums, springs, wheels and tiny hammers; clocks that filled the house with a cheerful 'tick-tock, tick-tock', as though its heart were beating.

"Hurry, Dodie!" Theo called to his sister who was trailing behind. She was gazing at a flock of birds, swinging on the wind like blown-about bits of cloth.

"It's getting dark," Theo shouted.

Dodie took no notice. Now she was singing to herself and pirouetting on the pavement. Dodie was seven, a red-haired, freckle-faced girl who seemed to fear nothing. Theo was older, but he was secretly afraid of the dark and found it easy to believe in ghosts. His mother said he had too much imagination. Theo couldn't help it.

"Afternoon, Theo!" said Mr Oak. His

grey scarf was pulled over his chin and his peaked cap shadowed his eyes. Every day he waited for Theo to pass his gate on the way home. The old man always had a strange tale or a funny story to tell. But today Mr Oak wasn't smiling. He looked as though he had something grim to say, a story Theo might not want to hear.

"How are you, Mr Oak?" Theo asked politely.

"Not so good, son. Not so good."

"What's the matter. Are you ill?"

"I've lost my cat, that's what," said Mr Oak. "I think a witch has stolen her."

"Why d'you say that?" asked Theo, trying not to sound alarmed.

"Because they're about, aren't they?" Mr Oak's voice was grave. "Witches always arrive in rough weather. They lose their

broomsticks and they lose their cats. So they come snooping around, trying to steal ours."

"Your cat will come back, Mr Oak," said Theo. "She's probably just exploring."

"Cats don't like the wind." Mr Oak looked up at a thrashing tree and Theo, following his glance, couldn't help shuddering.

"I thought I saw something over the wood," murmured the old man. "Nothing definite, mind. Could have been birds, you know how they look, all in a crowd, dark and winging. On the other hand…"

"Mr Oak," Theo broke in, "do witches look different from other people?"

"Not so's you'd notice. They're just like anyone else. Their clothes may be darker, and their skin more wrinkled from travelling in the wind. And there's always the hat, folded secretly into a pocket, when they don't want to be recognised."

Dodie had caught up with Theo and was listening with rapt attention to this talk of witches.

"There's no way, then, of telling who's a witch?" asked Theo.

"None at all, except…"

"Except?" Theo repeated urgently.

Mr Oak scratched a blue-tinged ear and drew his scarf closer round his neck. "They do say…" he cleared his throat while the children waited breathlessly. "They do say that witches' tears turn to crystal, as soon as they fall."

"Oooooh!" sighed Dodie. "I'd like to see them."

"Thing is," Mr Oak gave a grim smile, "witches don't cry, or hardly ever."

The children stared at Mr Oak's mysterious face, trying to guess what the look in his hooded eyes meant.

Suddenly Dodie cried, "Look! Hailstones!"

And there they were, tumbling out of the sky like fierce white pearls.

"We'd better get home," said Theo. "Mum's alone."

"How is Mrs Blossom?" asked the old man.

"Mum's all right, but Dad's away," Theo told him.

"And you're looking after the house and feel responsible?" said Mr Oak.

"I *am* responsible," said Theo.

The children ran on, calling goodbye to Mr Oak.

He waved and turned his attention to the sky again, guarding his face from the icy drops with a grey mittened hand.

The children's black cat, Flora, was waiting on the wall. Theo snatched her up and carried her indoors. His heart was beating fast. He told himself that he wasn't afraid of witches, and it was only the weather that worried him, but he clung to Flora even when he was safe inside.

Chapter Two

The kitchen was steamy and orange-scented. Mrs Blossom had been busy; pots of marmalade stood in rows, all along the dresser, on the kitchen table and even on the windowsill. Mr Blossom had a passion for marmalade.

"Your father's coming home tomorrow," Mrs Blossom told the children, "and there's a dance in the village hall."

"What'll you wear?" asked Dodie.

"I'm going to mend my old red dress. I can't afford to buy anything new."

Mr Blossom was often away. He travelled all over the country, visiting other people's clocks; grandfather clocks that wouldn't chime, china clocks that wouldn't tick, and golden ormolu clocks that lost the hours they were supposed to keep. Mr Blossom had a special way with time. He had never been late for a date with his wife.

"You look good in your red dress," said Theo. "No one would guess it was old."

"Yes, but I wish…" his mother sighed.

"What do you wish?" asked Dodie.

"It's our wedding anniversary," said Mrs Blossom, "and I'm going to look such a frump."

"Wear your crystal necklace," suggested Dodie. "Dad always says it makes you sparkle."

"If only I could," Mrs Blossom smiled awkwardly.

"Why can't you, Mum?" asked Theo.

"Well... I... I seem to have mislaid it."

"We'll find it," cried Dodie. "Won't we, Theo?"

"No, children..." began Mrs Blossom, but Dodie and Theo were already hunting. They searched the house from top to bottom, emptied drawers, cupboards, boxes and waste-paper baskets. They looked under the beds, the carpets, the sofa and the kitchen sink. Last of all they carefully moved the clocks, all except the grandfather, that stood gleaming splendidly in the hall. But the precious crystals were nowhere to be found.

"It can't be helped," said Mrs Blossom. "We'd better clear the table for tea."

Theo was hungry and would have come straight to the table, but something caught his eye. There, moving through the gate, was a shadowy rumpled figure. He wanted to pull the curtains against the mysterious shape, but he was afraid to go too near the window. Perhaps if he turned his back, the 'thing' would just go away. Then Dodie saw it.

"Look," she cried. "There's a bundle of something outside. The hailstones have driven it into our garden."

A dark figure whirled up to the window, flapping its arms like a bird.

"It wants to come in," said Dodie.

"Don't let it, Mum," Theo murmured.

At first, Mrs Blossom, peering at the windowpane, could only see reflected jars of marmalade winking at her. Then she glimpsed a white face and a waving arm.

"Someone needs help," she exclaimed. "A poor old soul has been caught in the weather." And she went to open the door.

The children followed her, and found a dark bundle drooping on the step.

"Can I help you?" asked Mrs Blossom.

Theo whispered, "No, Mum. It might not be friendly!"

But his mother had already stepped back and the stranger was hobbling into their home. When she passed Theo she darted a look at him, from under her black hood. Her cunning eyes were jackdaw grey and Theo felt trapped by them, like a rabbit caught in the glare of a stoat. And he thought of Mr Oak's dire warning, about witches arriving in rough weather.

Chapter Three

"Come and sit by the stove," said Mrs Blossom, ignoring Theo's tug at her sleeve. "It's not the weather for travelling. Have you lost your way?"

"Uh-huh!" creaked the voice.

Theo heard a moan like old ships' timbers, as the stranger bent herself into a chair. He moved a bit closer and dared to ask, "Where were you going?"

"Nowhere special," said the old woman.

"Just out for an airing."

"And you got lost?"

"Not exactly, dear. I just fell off..."

"Fell off what?" asked Dodie and Theo together.

"I fell off the kerb, dears. Such slippery weather. It's given my bones a terrible shaking."

Theo thought: fell off a broomstick, more like.

"You haven't seen a cat, have you?" asked the old woman. "A big black tom?"

The children shook their heads, and Theo looked round anxiously for Flora.

"You'll want some tea, I'm sure," said Mrs Blossom, filling the kettle again. "I'm Mrs Blossom, and you are...?"

"Scarum's the name." The old woman smiled, revealing a single tooth like an icicle in a dark cave. "I'd love a cuppa."

"Scarum? An unusual name," Mrs Blossom remarked.

"A witch's name," Theo whispered.

"You can't scare me," hissed Dodie.

"Children, it's rude to whisper," said their mother. "Do something to help. Take Mrs Scarum's coat and hang it near the stove."

When Theo touched the black coat, it slithered between his fingers like the silky skin of a mole. As he draped it on the back of a chair, he noticed a tiny disturbance in the ticking of the carved wooden clock on the mantelpiece behind him. It was as if it had been surprised for a moment and couldn't compose itself. And then, when all the other clocks chimed the half-hour, the wooden clock couldn't catch up. It strained and whirred, making a fool of itself, a thing that had never happened before.

"What a tick-tock room," said Mrs Scarum, gazing round with her jackdaw eyes.

"My husband mends clocks," Mrs Blossom explained, handing her guest a cup of tea. "People say he has a magic touch. Not one has ever defeated him."

"My, my!" said Mrs Scarum. "Time's a precious thing – to some."

"But not to you," said Theo.

Mrs Scarum made no reply. She just sipped her tea and smiled, showing her single tooth again. And then Flora walked in and the old woman's grey eyes glittered as she watched the cat settle herself by the stove. "What a beauty," she murmured hungrily.

"She's not good with strangers." Theo scooped up Flora and hugged her tight.

"Theo! She's never hurt a soul," his mother said reproachfully. "She has the sweetest nature."

Too sweet, thought Theo.

"If you don't live far away, Mrs Scarum, I'll take you home when you've had another cup of tea," offered Mrs Blossom.

"Ooooooo!" The visitor let out a wail.

"Not yet! I'd like a bite to eat if it's not too much trouble. Toad-in-the-hole's my favourite."

Mrs Blossom looked perplexed and Theo wondered if there was enough food in the house for four. "I'll borrow some sausages," his mother said, deciding to do all she could for the stranger. "Mrs Bellinger over the road always has plenty to spare. I won't be a second."

"And while you're out I'll bake a cake!" announced Mrs Scarum.

"There's really no need..." Mrs Blossom was flustered.

"It's the least I can do," their visitor insisted. "Your little girl will show me where you keep the flour."

"Yes, yes!" cried Dodie. "I love making cakes."

Mrs Blossom wrapped herself in a scarf and coat, and ran into the blustery street, while Dodie began to open cupboards. "Sugar, eggs, jam and flour," she chanted. "A bowl, a sieve, two spoons and a whisk!" The table was soon covered with all the things Dodie thought a cook might need.

"Now, shoo!" said Mrs Scarum. "This is going to be a surprise cake. No peeping while I work."

"A surprise," breathed Dodie, already half-covering her eyes. "Come on, Theo, let's watch TV until the surprise is ready."

But Theo waited just out of sight, or so he thought, behind the open door. He wanted to know what secret ingredients were going into this mysterious cake.

Mrs Scarum didn't weigh the flour like his mother did. She just tossed it carelessly

into the bowl, every scrap, until it rose in the air and filled the kitchen with drifting clouds. She juggled the eggs, four at a time, before breaking them into Mrs Blossom's best blue jug. And then she hunted through the cupboards, sniffing and humming.

At last she found a tiny bottle and brought it into the light. She gave a giggle of glee. It was Mr Blossom's precious clock oil, and Theo couldn't help a little gasp of surprise.

The old woman, squinting at the twilight-coloured windowpane, spied a shadowy reflection above the shining rows of marmalade: a boy and his cat. "Boy," she said. "Don't snoop. Just leave your cat and go."

"I won't leave my cat," said Theo.

Before he turned away he sneaked one quick look into the kitchen, and saw Mrs Scarum pull something from her pocket. Beside the big white mixing-bowl she laid a dark and crumpled object.

"A witch's hat," breathed Theo, tiptoeing away.

Chapter Four

Mrs Blossom came back in a flurry of hailstones. They followed her into the house and hid in corners, tiny pearls of ice trying not to melt.

Strange sounds spilled from the kitchen: a humming, chanting, chuckling breeze that washed through the house in eerie gusts. And in the background, spoons rattled, glass sang and leather boots drummed on the floorboards. Not exactly

27

the sounds of someone cooking.

"It's bitter outside," called Mrs Blossom, shaking the ice from her coat. "The weather's closing in. The roads are empty and... Oooooh!"

The children ran to see what had surprised their mother. A cake stood on the kitchen table; a layered white mountain with candles sparkling on the top. Painted on the side in scarlet icing was a name.

Flora!

"Happy birthday, Pussy!" sang Mrs Scarum.

"It's not Flora's birthday," Theo told her firmly.

"Just trying to be friendly," said the old woman.

"You're very kind!" Mrs Blossom flung off her coat and began to tidy away.

"How did you make a giant cake so fast?" asked Dodie, gazing at the sparkling monster.

"I've got cook's fingers," replied their visitor. "It's a gift."

"A spell, more like," Theo whispered close to Dodie's ear. "She's got a witch's hat."

"I told you not to try and scare me." Dodie gave Theo a shove. "There's no such thing as a witch."

Theo didn't argue. Mrs Scarum was staring at him and he couldn't tell if her glinting eyes were kind.

Mrs Blossom put the white cake beside the clock on the dresser and the clock gave a small whirring sigh, as if it were afraid of its giant neighbour. It was a china clock and Theo's favourite. It had a small round face set between a shepherd boy with a broken foot, and his one-eared, tail-less sheepdog. Theo thought the wounded shepherd probably enjoyed the cheerful beat of his clock. What would he do if the clock stopped ticking?

"Stop dreaming, Theo, and lay the table," said Mrs Blossom.

Theo didn't want to let Flora go, but she slipped out of his arms and ran to her favourite chair in the corner.

When they all sat down to tea Mrs Scarum attacked her toad-in-its-hole with relish. Dodie and Theo couldn't look at her; the noise she made was horrible. Her gums squelched and her tongue slid round her cavernous mouth, while her single tooth punctured the food in vicious snaps. They had almost finished the meal when the lights began to flicker.

"I must get some candles ready," said

Mrs Blossom. "There might be a power cut, the way the weather's going." She turned on the radio just in time to hear a voice advising people to stay at home. "There's a blizzard on the way," she said.

"Oh dear! Oh dear! I'll never get home," said Mrs Scarum through a mouthful of toad.

"But where *is* your home?" asked Theo.

"Too far," the old woman said. "I'll never get there in weather like this. I need... I need..."

A broomstick, Theo thought.

"A car's no use now," said his mother. "Blizzards are treacherous. You'd better spend the night with us, Mrs Scarum, and we'll get you home tomorrow."

"You're a dear," said the old woman, "a real treasure."

"I'm afraid we haven't a spare bed, but I can lend you a good warm nightie, and you can sleep on the sofa by the sitting-room fire." Mrs Blossom's busy chatter suddenly flagged as she caught sight of the wooden clock-face. And Theo saw it was nearly half-past six. His father always phoned at five. He'd never missed.

"Where is he?" Mrs Blossom murmured, and as she spoke the clocks all faltered. Just for a second they lost their rhythm. Tick-creak-tock went the wooden clock. Tick-wheeze-tock called the china shepherd. Tick-swish-tock mumbled the ormolu.

"Do you sleep well in a house full of ticking?" asked Mrs Scarum. "No offence. I just wondered."

"We're used to it," said Mrs Blossom. "It's comforting, especially when Mr Blossom's on his travels."

"Of course," the old woman said, and then added quickly, "my toes get so cold in winter. You'll let your little cat keep me warm tonight, won't you?"

"No! No! No!" protested Theo. "Don't let her!"

"What's got into you?" his mother

complained. "Shouting like that. It's rude."

"But Flora belongs to me," Theo protested.

"Flora belongs to no one," Mrs Scarum leant close to him. "A cat goes where it wants to. You can't make it stay. It's got a powerful will, has a cat."

Theo was struck dumb. He looked round desperately, to see if Flora was safe. But there she was, curled in her chair and purring gently.

Mrs Blossom offered her guest a hot water bottle, but Mrs Scarum wasn't happy. "It's not the same as a cat," she grumbled.

If only she'd go, thought Theo. If only the blizzard would turn away and let her go back to where she came from. If only Dad were here. He turned to the shepherd clock, wishing its hands would tell him it was morning, and there was still a chance that the day would be fine, and a mysterious stranger wouldn't be forced to shelter in their home.

How can I tell if our guest is a witch, wondered Theo, *if witches hardly ever cry?* Once again he felt the clocks hesitate, and there was a curious bend in time, a tock-ticking, un-winding of confused springs and pendulums. And he thought of his father, whose heart beat like a clock. Why hadn't he phoned? Was he caught somewhere on an icy road, or lost on the moor and slowly freezing?

Chapter Five

Mrs Blossom began to pile blankets on to the sofa. When the children looked into the living-room, there was a soft white pillow tucked at one end, and a long creamy nightdress laid over the arm.

Mrs Scarum held up the nightdress and began to dance with it. The cotton billowed round her as she pranced about the house, and Theo marvelled at her energy. "Aren't I pretty?" she sang.

"Oh yes," said Dodie, but Theo, who preferred to be honest, said nothing.

"Come on, Theo, what do you think?" asked Mrs Scarum, pouting.

"I think you look... unusual," said Theo.

"You don't believe I was once a beauty, then?"

"I didn't say that," answered Theo.

"I'll tell you a story," their visitor offered, bouncing down on the sofa.

"It's just the weather for stories," said Dodie, happily settling in beside Mrs Scarum.

"Have you heard the one about the rainbow that climbed so high it spun all the way out to the stars?"

"Tell us!" cried Dodie. "Now!"

"Rainbows don't come at night," muttered Theo, and he went to look out of the window.

The old woman began her tale in a

funny, sing-song, story-telling voice. While she talked, Mrs Blossom popped in and out of the room carrying comforts for her visitor: a glass of water, a pair of bedsocks, a night-light in a saucer. She was always doing things for other people, in her shy, gentle way. And Theo wished that one day someone would reward her for her kindness.

Now Mrs Scarum was telling a different story. Although Theo didn't want to go too near the old woman, he found himself drawn by the jangly voice, and before he knew it, his arms were on the back of the sofa and he was leaning close to the frosty white head. Mrs Scarum was telling Dodie about a time, long ago, when a blizzard had come, so fierce, so cold and heavy, that everything stopped moving. And a young man on his way home was caught where he stood, lost in the snow and still calling. "He looked like a youth made of ice, when they found him," said the old voice. "His blue eyes were open, still searching the snow for a path."

"How sad," said Dodie with a shiver.

Just then Flora walked in and sat beside the fire. A wrinkled hand slipped from the folds of a skirt and reached out to welcome her.

"Flora, come here!" said Theo sharply.

Flora pushed her head against Mrs Scarum's bony fingers, and purred.

"She likes me," the old woman said.

And suddenly the clocks began to chime; a loud, desperate ringing filled the house. Springs whined, pendulums swung and bells pealed.

"One-two-three-four," Theo counted, "five-six-seven." But the sound was uneven and out of tune. The clocks were losing time.

"It's late!" Theo cried. "Too late! Where's Dad?"

"Where should he be?" asked Mrs Scarum.

"Somewhere safe," said Theo, "where there's a telephone. He always rings at five. What's happened?"

"He's delayed, dear. Ice slows people down. Or it could be the telegraph poles, cracked by the blizzard, wires all snapped. Dangerous things, if you ask me, stretched across the land like that, all those wires higgledy-piggledy."

"Dangerous?" said Theo.

"To the birds, dear," Mrs Scarum told him, "and other... flying things."

Like you, thought Theo, who could imagine Mrs Scarum flying on a broomstick, enjoying the freedom of the sky and possibly the company of a big black cat, until W-H-O-O-S-H, she's blown off course, straight into the path of those wicked black wires. Over goes the broomstick, down goes the witch, away goes the cat.

"You mustn't fret, dear," said Mrs Scarum, mistaking his anxious expression. "Tell old Scarum your troubles."

"I'm worried for Mum," Theo confessed, but he wouldn't say more than that. It was Dodie who told the old woman about their mother's lost necklace, the dance in the village, and their father's long journey over the moor.

"A necklace, you say?" Mrs Scarum scratched her bristly chin.

"It's their wedding anniversary," said Dodie. "And Mum wanted to sparkle. Tell me another story, Mrs Scarum. Please, before I go to bed."

Theo went to find his mother. She was in the kitchen, watching the shepherd-boy clock.

"What d'you think's happened to Dad?" he asked. "Is it the blizzard, Mum?"

"It must be," she said.

"Do blizzards stop clocks?"

"Not these clocks, Theo. They aren't electric. They're old, but they're strong, and they've always kept perfect time, ever since your father's had them."

"But supposing he's lost," whispered Theo. "There'd be no one to keep them going.

Perhaps they know that he's in trouble and they're afraid of dying!"

His mother smiled at him. It was a brave but anxious smile, and when the wind gave an icy howl, she threw a desperate glance at the window. And Theo almost told Mrs Scarum's story about the young man turned to ice, with his blue eyes still open, searching the snow for a path.

But he kept the story to himself.

Chapter six

At bedtime, Theo tucked Flora under his arm and carried her upstairs.

"Couldn't she stay?" called Mrs Scarum. "To keep an old woman warm?"

"No," said Theo sternly. He put Flora in Dodie's doll's cradle and covered her with a blanket. Flora had always liked that. She didn't even mind when the cradle was gently rocked.

"Mum won't let her stay," warned Dodie.

"She doesn't like cats in bedrooms at night."

"She must let her stay," said Theo. "Otherwise someone will steal her."

"Who?"

"Who d'you think. Witches need cats, especially black ones."

"If you mean Mrs Scarum, that's silly. She's just a poor old woman who likes cats."

Dodie's been won over by her stories, that grand cake and a silly dance with a white nightdress, thought Theo.

"Think what you like," he said. "I can read the signs. And Mr Oak warned us." He heard his mother's footsteps on the stairs and putting a finger to his lips he whispered, "Don't tell Mum about Flora, Dodie!"

"All right," she agreed. "But I still don't believe in witches."

When Mrs Blossom came in she didn't notice Flora in the cradle. Her thoughts seemed far away, and tiny lines on her forehead gave her face a bothered and unhappy look.

"Dad still hasn't phoned, has he, Mum?" said Theo.

His mother shook her head. "But we mustn't worry, Theo. The weather's worse in the north. He's probably sheltering in a little hotel where the phone doesn't work and the lights are out, but it'll be warm and friendly all the same."

Theo could tell that his mother didn't believe her own words. "And what about the clocks, Mum?" he asked. "What if they don't work, in the place where Dad's staying?"

"Then your father will mend them, won't

he?" Mrs Blossom smiled at last. "Your father always knows the time. He'll be back tomorrow, just you see." She kissed the children goodnight and turned to go, but a peaceful purr from the corner made her stop and peer into the doll's cradle. "Tch! Tch! You know Flora can't sleep up here!" she said.

"But it's safer, Mum," Theo pleaded.

"Don't be silly, Theo. She'll be safe in her basket by the stove. The blizzard can't hurt her."

"It's not the blizzard," muttered Theo.

Mrs Blossom shook her head, but as she bent over Flora's cradle, the grandfather clock at the foot of the stairs gave a hollow chime. The other clocks followed, one by one, a musical pattern that was losing its way, tolling feebly against the sound of the wind that was trying to smother it.

Mrs Blossom sat back on Dodie's bed as if she too were being wound down by the blizzard.

"Don't worry, Mum!" Dodie hugged her mother. "It'll be just like you said, I know it will. Dad will come home with a pile of old clocks ticking in the back of his van. And you'll go to the dance, and we'll find the necklace, and tomorrow you'll sparkle."

"Oh, Dodie," said Mrs Blossom sadly. "You'll never find it."

"Of course we will," insisted Dodie.

"I'm sorry," said Mrs Blossom. "It'll just be a waste of time." She looked so forlorn Theo exclaimed, "It can't just disappear."

"It hasn't disappeared," said Mrs Blossom softly.

"Then where is it?" asked Theo.

"I sold my lucky necklace," his mother declared in a rush, "and maybe I'll never sparkle again."

"You sold it?" cried Theo in alarm. "But why?"

"We needed the money, Theo. We had bills to pay. Last month the roof was repaired, and Dad's van needed servicing. He hasn't been doing so well lately."

"But you let us look for it," Dodie

grumbled, "all over the house."

"I'm sorry. I didn't want to tell you the truth."

"It's better than lies," said Theo angrily. "You should never have sold it. That necklace was special."

"Of course it was. But I had no choice." Mrs Blossom pushed back her hair with a weary sigh.

"It was your lucky necklace," said Dodie gravely. "What will happen to us without it?"

"We'll find luck somewhere else." The words were comforting but her voice was wan. And Theo felt sorry for being angry. He pulled the bedclothes over his head and heard his mother walk away. She had forgotten all about Flora.

"Theo, wake up," came a whisper, when the house was quiet.

Theo wasn't asleep. His eyes were closed, but he couldn't stop his mind from racing. He was wondering why the clocks were so troubled, wondering where his father was, why he hadn't phoned and whether the old woman was really a witch.

"What is it?" he asked.

"She wouldn't really steal Flora, would she?" asked Dodie. "The old woman, I mean. She seems so kind."

"Huh! That's just a trick," Theo told her. "They pretend to be ever so sweet and old and nice. And then bang!" He snapped his fingers. "They're gone with your cat and your money, and whatever else they want."

"D'you really think their tears are made of crystal?"

"It's what old Mr Oak said. But don't

ask me how you can make a witch cry. They're too hard-hearted."

"Not Mrs Scarum," Dodie was firm. "I saw a tear in the corner of her eye when I talked about Mum's necklace and Dad being lost."

"He isn't lost," said Theo desperately. "And she'd hardly cry over someone else's troubles. Now go to sleep."

But Dodie wasn't in the mood for sleep. "Witches aren't always bad," she murmured. "Sometimes they help."

"Not Mrs Scarum," argued Theo, "with her shifty eyes and her patchy face. She's full of trickery and cunning. I can tell."

"You can't," said Dodie. "You can only see the outside of her, the part that's old. Behind her skin she might be beautiful."

"Huh!" Theo wriggled under the covers

and turned his back on Dodie. He could hear her talking away to herself, while the wind wailed and hailstones rapped on the windowpane. At last, his sister's voice grew quiet, the storm died and Theo fell asleep.

While the children dreamed, something called Flora out of her sleep. She jumped from the cradle and ran to the open bedroom door. She stopped, one paw raised in hesitation, and turned her sleek black head to catch the drift of a message meant only for her. She answered with a soft mew, then sped soundlessly down the dark stairwell, and into the room where a window had been left open, ready to let her out.

Chapter seven

When Theo looked out of the window next morning, the ground was covered with snow, but the sky was blue again. It was Saturday.

Pulling on clothes as fast as he could, he ran downstairs. His mother and Dodie were in the kitchen, already halfway through their breakfast, and Mrs Scarum was sitting by the stove in his mother's red dressing-gown.

"We let you sleep, Theo," said Mrs Blossom.

"Dodie tells me you were tossing and turning all night."

"Was I?" mumbled Theo, with a look at Mrs Scarum. The old woman smiled, but didn't say a word.

"We've washed Mrs Scarum's muddy clothes," explained his mother. "There's a wonderful breeze for drying."

Theo sat down at the table, and then something made him ask, "Where's Flora?"

"Can't find her," said Dodie, munching cornflakes.

"What?" cried Theo, leaping up.

"I called her," said Dodie, "but she never came."

"No!" shouted Theo. "She's been stolen, or... or worse."

"Calm down, Theo," said Mrs Blossom. "Of course she hasn't been stolen. She likes to go off and explore, sometimes."

"But there's snow on the ground," he moaned. "She'll never find her way home, and supposing the blizzard comes back." He stared accusingly at Mrs Scarum, who turned her face away and held her bony fingers over the stove.

"She's had a spell put on her," Theo went on, and he ran into the sitting-room to see if Flora was hiding there. The windows were firmly fastened, but just beneath the sill he noticed a little pile of hailstones. Had the windows been opened in the night? Perhaps. And yet the warmth of the room hadn't melted the ice.

Through the window he could see Mrs Scarum's dark clothes flapping on the line, even her black woollen stockings had been washed. *When the clothes are dry perhaps*

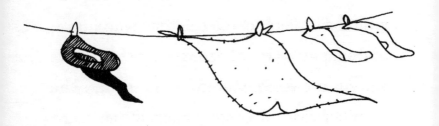

she'll be off, thought Theo, *and we'll be safe again.*

He trailed back into the kitchen. "Flora's lost," he said. "I'm sure of it." Over by the stove something rang on the hard tiles, like glass bouncing. And he saw that Mrs Scarum was wiping her eyes with a handkerchief.

"I'm so sorry," the old woman spoke with a catch in her voice. "Poor Flora. I hope all is well with her." There it was again, a soft clink on the floor. A tiny crystal rolled under the table just as they saw the milkman approaching the house in a haze of flying ice, which began to rap relentlessly against the windowpane.

When Mrs Blossom opened the front door, hailstones poured into the house while the milkman stood laughing. "It's spooky weather," he said. "Whatever next? I see the van's gone. I hope Mr Blossom's all right."

"I don't know where he is," Mrs Blossom told him.

Seeing her anxious face, the milkman said quickly, "Don't worry now, Mrs Blossom. Your husband's safe. The snow's just held him up a bit."

She smiled, a little desperately, and closed the door against another surge of ice. Then out she ran, into the back garden to tug Mrs Scarum's clothes off the line, raced into the kitchen with her dark armful and hung them, skirt, stockings and long woolly cardigan, over the stove. "They'll dry there," she said, almost too brightly.

And all the while Mrs Scarum sat gazing at the stove and rubbing her hands together, slowly, very slowly, as a soundless trickle of tears slid down her leathery cheeks.

Clink! Clink! On to the tiles. Something hit the floor with a shrill patter. Ice on stone.

"Oh, no!" cried Mrs Blossom. "The window frame's loose. I knew we should have fixed it before winter. Look, the hailstones are getting in."

"Flora might freeze if the weather goes bad again," said Dodie. And Theo muttered under his breath, "Our dad might be frozen already." He knew what his mother was thinking. Why didn't the telephone ring?

Mrs Scarum began to mutter in a thin, wheezy voice. "She can't be lost. I meant no harm. I asked her to look for something. I had a cat. A big black tom called Harum. What a team! Harum and Scarum. A brave cat, a beautiful cat. Perhaps he's lost too," and drops of crystal rattled to the floor, faster and faster.

"The weather's breaking in on us," cried Mrs Blossom. "It's following me. Sweep it up, children, or we'll have a lake in here."

"Two lost cats," said Dodie. "Perhaps they'll find each other."

But Theo, pushing a broom over the tiles, thought: *These drops of ice aren't going to melt*. And Dodie, sweeping the glittering pile into a dustpan, muttered, "They're hard as crystal!" She opened the window and poured them out, but as they lay there, sparkling up at her, they began to fill with rainbow colours, as though someone had scattered a handful of jewels across the snow.

Chapter Eight

Mrs Scarum's steaming clothes filled the kitchen with strange scents. Gone was the warm tang of oranges; now the room was awash with pine and nightshade.

Theo was asked to polish Mrs Scarum's boots, while Dodie stirred the soup. "Our visitor must have something warm before she starts her journey," Mrs Blossom said.

But would there be a journey? Theo wondered. Perhaps Mrs Scarum didn't want to leave. The old woman sat by the fire all morning, in her borrowed dressing-gown. And when the soup was served she sipped it very slowly, making one spoonful last as long as five. No one knew what to say. The wind began to whine again, then snow fluttered against the window.

"I don't feel so good," murmured Mrs Scarum. "Perhaps I could rest for a while." Her grey eyes flitted round the table, daring them to refuse her.

"It'd be better to travel in daylight," said Theo sternly.

His mother frowned at him. "Of course you can rest, Mrs Scarum," she said, as she helped her visitor back into the sitting-room.

"She'll never go," hissed Theo when his mother came back. "She's settling deeper and deeper into our house. We'll never be able to get her out."

"Nonsense, Theo. Mrs Scarum's very old and quite exhausted. You saw how upset she was just now. It won't hurt to let her stay another night."

"Another night?" cried Theo. "No, Mum!"

"Theo, what is it?" said Mrs Blossom. "It's not like you to be so unkind."

"But I'm worried, Mum," said Theo helplessly. "I can't help it."

"He thinks Mrs Scarum's a witch," said Dodie with a giggle.

Theo glared at her, feeling betrayed. "But there is *something*," he said earnestly. "You can't say there isn't. The clocks aren't working properly; they're so tired, it's like they're dying. Perhaps Mrs Scarum's doing something to them, and where's Flora? She's always here for her breakfast."

"Calm down, Theo," Mrs Blossom told him gently. "It's only the weather. It does peculiar things."

The snow kept falling for the rest of the day. Inch by inch, layer upon layer. An eerie whiteness smothered the village. Each house was an island in a pale, hushed sea.

Theo, watching from the window, didn't think the snow was beautiful. He felt like someone drowning. Even Dodie was subdued. She took a cup of tea in to their visitor, but found her fast asleep.

"Then don't disturb her," said Mrs Blossom. "She needs her sleep," as though the old woman was weakening by the minute, along with the drowsy clocks.

It was the strangest day Theo could ever remember. The snow didn't draw them out to play, it seemed to keep them prisoner. Every hour he would go and call to Flora, but by nightfall she still hadn't returned.

Dodie fell asleep as soon as she got to bed, all the chatter drained out of her. But Theo lay awake for hours, knowing that things were not right. At last he slipped out of bed and tiptoed over to the door. An eerie, out-of-place whisper crept along the dark passage towards him. But nothing stirred. The house was silent yet not at peace. He felt for the light switch and pressed it quickly. Nothing happened. So the power had been cut. And yet the house wasn't dark. It was filled with a pale, mysterious light. Theo made his way to the staircase and began to descend. The sound of old wood creaking under his feet was comforting.

When he was halfway down the stairs he paused and listened again. Nothing. And then he knew what was wrong. The peaceful rhythm of the house had been broken. The clocks had all stopped ticking.

Chapter Nine

Theo could have turned back or called to his mother. He could have stayed where he was, breathless and frightened on the stairs. But he found himself stepping down into the hall, where the grandfather clock stood, tall and mute.

As Theo passed the clock he glanced up at its lifeless hands. "What's happening?" he asked in a hushed voice. The clock gazed out helplessly, as if to say, "Someone has stolen my breath."

So Theo pressed on, into the room where he thought a witch was sleeping. Firelight flickered on rumpled blankets and a snow-white pillow, but Mrs Scarum's makeshift bed was empty. And then Theo saw a figure standing by the window.

All at once the moon sailed into view, and the figure was bathed in silver. She was upright and slender, and pale hair fell over her shoulders. The voice, when it came, was soft and tuneful. "Are you afraid, Theo?"

Too frightened to lie, he said, "Yes," in a choked sort of voice. "Everything's wrong."

"Not wrong, Theo. Just waiting."

"What for?" he whispered.

"For things to come right."

"The clocks have all stopped. Are they waiting?"

"You could say that. Their hearts won't beat again until your father is safe."

The voice began to hum a lullaby, and its gentle rhythm seemed to replace the constant beat of the clocks, the pulse that kept the house alive. Theo felt as though his life too depended on the tranquil song. He asked no questions but stood, patiently waiting. He became aware that a voice was telling him a story that he'd heard before, only this time the story came alive inside his head, and he saw a young man caught in a cloud of crystals, a young man with glazed blue eyes and a call for help frozen on his lips.

"He was my husband," said the gentle voice, "and I lost him. It shan't happen to your father, Theo. I promise you."

"But how…?" Theo began.

"Lucky black cats. They'll see him through…" the voice trailed off until it sounded like the wind far, far away.

The moon began to disappear and a breeze whistled past the house. A dark cloud boiled over the horizon, and with a crash, the window burst open and a shower of hailstones rattled into the room.

Theo fled, up the stairs, two at a time, stumbling and thumping along the darkening passage and into bed.

"What's happening, where have you been?" cried Dodie, waking up.

From beneath his pillow, Theo's muffled voice said, "Nowhere, Dodie. Hide your eyes. You must go to sleep."

Dodie turned over, too dozy to argue. Soon she was dreaming again, and so was Theo.

Chapter Ten

Deep in sleep Theo dreamed that he was very, very cold. Everything his closed eyes showed him was veiled in glinting white. He was travelling up an icy lane and out on to the wide, frozen moor, where a green van coughed and struggled against the weather.

A man got out of the van. Mr Blossom in his hooded brown coat and the long blue scarf that matched the colour of his eyes, so Mrs Blossom said. The wind tore at his coat and hurled snow in his face as his blue eyes searched the bleak white moor. And then, in a gesture that frightened Theo more than anything, Mr Blossom covered his face with his hands. And Theo knew his father was lost and afraid.

"Help!" Theo cried in his sleep. But who could help. The moor was deserted. Not a soul would have stirred on such a treacherous night. And Theo couldn't reach his father, couldn't touch him. Mr Blossom was alone in the blizzard. Or was he?

Gradually the air around Mr Blossom became quite still. He let his hands fall and stared at something that moved through the frosty night. Walking towards him were two coal-black cats. The larger cat walked like a panther, the other was smaller and dainty. Placing paws carefully into the snow the

cats made a path that could clearly be seen as a narrow track that wound into the distance behind them. The cats stopped a few feet from the van. Mysterious eyes blazed at Mr Blossom, so fierce and bright that sleeping Theo was dazzled by them. The creatures then turned away and walked back down the path they had just made through the snow. But before they disappeared they looked back as if to say, "Follow our trail, we're here to help."

Mr Blossom climbed into the green van. The engine started and the van moved after the black cats.

It was many hours later when Theo woke up and found himself safe in bed. Sunlight glowed behind the curtains, and the house was filled with the sound of chiming clocks.

Chapter Eleven

Mrs Scarum joined the family for breakfast. She seemed quite her old self again. Grey eyes full of mischief and a curious titter spilling over her teacup.

The house had got its rhythm back and all the clocks were merrily ticking.

When Theo went to fetch a bowl from the larder, the white cake towered before him. But now it bore a different message. "Welcome Home," said the scarlet icing. Theo slammed the larder door. What did the message mean?

He had just poured milk on to his cornflakes when the back door burst open with a crash.

"Dodie, you didn't latch it properly," grumbled Mrs Blossom.

"I did," said Dodie, and then she dropped her spoon as Flora walked into the room. "You clever, clever cat," cried Dodie, scooping up Flora and hugging her tight. "How did you open the door?"

But Flora wasn't alone. Into the kitchen came the biggest, shiniest cat they had ever seen. And yet... and yet, to Theo he looked familiar.

"Harum!" screeched Mrs Scarum. She fell on the monster's neck, laughing and crying as a stream of hailstones rushed

through the open door, bouncing against the walls, tinkling on the china and rolling across the floor. Everywhere Theo looked, beads of crystal whirled and spun.

"Our room looks like a snowstorm," he said. "The sort they keep in little glass domes and then turn upside down and shake."

"The blizzard's come back and the sun is shining," said Dodie. "What a wonky world." She gathered a handful and spun them over her head, singing, "Icicle Rain! Look how it's shining!"

Mrs Blossom ran round with a dustpan, slipping on the glassy tears, and pouring them out of the window as fast as she could. Theo helped with a broom and a bucket, while Mrs Scarum clung to her Harum, tears trickling down her crinkled cheeks.

And then the telephone rang!

Theo and Dodie waited, hardly daring to breathe, while their mother raced to answer the call. Even Mrs Scarum was quiet. The two cats beamed secret messages at one another.

A joyful shout came from the hall.

"It's Dad," guessed Theo. "Everything's safe now."

"Hooray!" cried Dodie.

"Your father's on his way," Mrs Blossom called out. "But he's got such a strange story to tell you."

Mrs Scarum smiled in a mysterious way, hiding the icicle tooth. "There," she said, "and a cake all ready to welcome him. We must be on our way, Harum and I. I feel so much better now."

"I'll iron your clothes," Mrs Blossom insisted.

Once more Theo and Dodie cleared the kitchen of hailstones. And as they carried them into the garden in buckets and bowls, Dodie whispered, "Will they melt, Theo?"

"I don't think I want to know." He poured his bucketful into a stream of melting snow that was running past the gate.

Mr Oak waved to them from the street. "What a blizzard," he called. "Never known anything like it, not in all my eighty years."

"Has your cat come back?" asked Theo.

"She was hiding under my bed. Just like a cat, to hide when the going gets rough."

"Not like Flora," said Dodie. "She's brave. She was out all night."

"Oh, ho." Mr Oak wagged a finger. "Remember what I said about witches."

"We do," said Theo, "but witches don't scare us."

"You wait till you meet one!"

The children didn't answer. They ran back into the house and found Mrs Scarum admiring herself in the hall mirror. "Don't I look grand," she said, dancing over the carpet. Mended and ironed, her skirt looked almost new. Her boots had been polished to

a brilliant shine and when she moved they could see that, here and there, a tiny star glittered on her velvety coat.

"You're a gem," Mrs Scarum declared, hugging the children's mother. "And now I must sniff the weather."

Dodie and Theo followed her outside. The wind was holding its breath, but the clouds were so low over the wood, you could hardly tell where the trees ended.

"Perfect," said Mrs Scarum. "I'll be off now, dears. I'll go the back way so the neighbours don't see me. There's an old man down your road who could give a person a bad reputation. That Mr Oak's got some funny ideas."

"I hope you get home before dark," said Theo.

"We're not afraid of the dark," tittered the old woman. "Are we, Harum?"

The big cat yawned disdainfully. He wasn't afraid of anything. Flora gazed at him with her honey-coloured eyes.

"There's just one thing." Mrs Scarum pulled on a long woollen hat. Was the end pointed, or was it round? "I need a stick. D'you think your mum...?"

"I'll fetch it," said Theo. "But first, will you tell me something."

The old woman cocked her head. "Well?"

"Would a witch take someone else's cat?"

"The very idea!" Mrs Scarum tickled her cat between the ears. "Witches have their own cats, I should imagine. They might send them off to do errands now and then, but the cats would always come back."

"I see." Theo ran inside and asked his mother for a walking stick.

"She must have the best," Mrs Blossom said, and she gave Theo a stout blackthorn that had belonged to her father. "She can keep it for as long as she wants. We'll see her again, some day."

"I wonder," said Theo.

Mrs Scarum was pleased with the stick. She tested it on the brittle snow and declared it just right for her purpose. "I'll send your mother something special," she told them.

The children were about to ask what it might be when a curious gust of wind blew out of the wood. The back gate swung open with a clatter as the draught rushed over the snow. It plucked at Mrs Scarum's skirt and she reeled round, laughing. Then she began to whirl across the ground. Cat, stick and old woman became a spinning pillar, a column of velvet and fur with, here and there, a green eye, a glimmering star, a pale hand waving and a touch of jackdaw grey.

She whisked through the gate and into the wood. The tall trees heaved a sigh and rustled uneasily.

"Goodbye," Theo murmured. "Go carefully!" And Flora, by his side, regarded the trees in a puzzled way and called out mournfully.

"Don't cry, Flora!" said Dodie. "You'll see him again one snowy day."

Chapter Twelve

A flock of crows rose out of the wood and fluttered up through the darkening sky, sending a flurry of snow in their wake. Soft as feathers, the snowflakes whirled over the garden and began to settle on the children. They spread their arms, hoping to look like snowmen, but the wind turned sharper, and the snow rushed at them in icy clouds. And something sparkled in the snow; a circle of tiny stars whirled down from the sky. It fell at Dodie's feet. An icy necklace filled with rainbow colours.

Dodie picked up the glistening string. "Look," she said. "Crystals."

Theo touched them gently. "Witch's tears," he murmured. "Threaded on silver."

"They're more beautiful than the ones Mum lost," Dodie said.

"Sold," Theo corrected her. "They must be from Mrs Scarum. Will Mum believe they're for her?"

They ran inside and Dodie held the crystals out to her mother. "Mrs Scarum's sent you something to wear," she said. "Now you can sparkle again."

Mrs Blossom's eyes were so bright, she was already sparkling. She took the necklace and unfastened the silver clasp. Then she held the crystals up to her throat and turned to her reflection in the windowpane.

"Do you believe in witches, Mum?" asked Theo.

"Do you?" echoed Dodie.

Mrs Blossom wouldn't answer her children, but her reflection looked out from the magic tears, and smiled at them.

Beyond the gate a green van drew up and a man got out. He wore a brown hooded coat and his eyes were as blue as the sky.

MORE THAN A STORY

CONTENTS PAGE

Theo's cat is on the prowl! Keep your eyes peeled and count how many pawprints you can find on these pages. (The answer's on the last page)

Which Witch?

How do you spot if someone is a witch?
There are different kinds of witches – bad witches,
good witches, beautiful witches and hideous witches.
Here are 10 signs that many years ago, people
believed would 'prove' that someone had extra
magic powers…

Witches:

1 are mostly women.

2 have special pets, like black cats or toads.

3 have moles or special marks on their skin.

4 mutter spells under their breath all the
time.

5 have special knowledge about medicine
and healing.

6 live alone.

7 don't cut their hair.

8 have no shadow.

9 can't drown in water.

10 are just different. Perhaps they cry tears of pure crystal?

What do you call a nervous witch?
A twitch

What happens if you see twin witches?
You can't tell which witch is witch!

WITCH SLIME

This is easy to make and looks disgusting...

You need:

225g cornstarch
half a pint of water
food colouring
1 adult

What you do:

1. Get the adult to boil the water in a pan and add
   the cornstarch. Ask them to mix it thoroughly and
   add a few drops of food colouring. Choose which
   colour you want. Green looks great – or purple.
   You can even mix the two.

2. Wait until the slime has cooled and is safe to touch!

3. Now squidge it between your fingers. You can add glitter if you like for a really bizarre effect.

A witch has passed this way and left a secret message. Unscramble the words to find what she's up to.

Srm umrasc si dninmge reh mscborotki.

Mrs Scarum is mending her broomstick.

Why did the witch give up fortune telling?
There was no future in it!

What do you call two witches who share a broomstick?
Broom-mates!

Witches in History

Many years ago, women were called 'witches' by their enemies simply because they were unusual in some way. It might be because they knew about healing herbs. Or it might just be because they were old or defenceless. Here are some famous witches from folklore, myth and history.

Circe

Circe was a beautiful witch who tricked men into eating a delicious meal which she had enchanted with a magic potion. It made them turn into animals. The Greek hero Odysseus rescued his men when they had been turned into pigs, by using a special plant, which some people say was a snowdrop.

Baba Yaga

Baba Yaga was a scary Russian witch who was supposed to travel around in a pestle and mortar, sweeping the way clear behind her with a broomstick. She lived in a house that stood on chicken's legs and kidnapped children if she got the chance.

Anne Boleyn

Anne Boleyn was married to King Henry VIII, and her daughter was to become a Queen – Elizabeth I. Anne's enemies said she was a witch because she had a sixth finger on one hand and because she had a large mole on her neck. Perhaps they were also jealous of her power over the King!

Morgan Le Fay

Morgan le Fay was said to be a witch. She was also the half-sister of King Arthur of the Knights of the Round Table. Although she was always causing trouble for much of Arthur's life, she took him away to the Isle of Avalon when he was fatally wounded in his last battle.

Find the Witch's Hat

Mrs Scarum is very forgetful. She's lost her hat in the Black Cat Estate and she can't remember where she's dropped it. Can you help her find it? You must keep to the open fly paths.

Why didn't the witch want to sing?
She had a frog in her throat.

Hair Scare!

To grow your very own witch's hair, you will need:

An egg
Cotton wool
Felt-tip pen
Cress seeds

What you do:

1 Get someone to help you break the top off a raw egg. Tip out the egg and save for another use. Now rinse out the egg shell with water.

2 Put your egg shell in an egg cup and draw a witch's face. Make it as scary as you can.

3 Fill the egg shell with damp cotton wool almost up to the top.

4 Sprinkle cress seeds on the cotton wool.

5 Now put the egg somewhere warm and dark until the first shoots start to appear. Don't forget to add a little water now and again.

6 Move to a sunny spot and watch the hair-do grow!

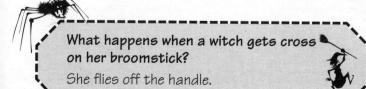

What happens when a witch gets cross on her broomstick?

She flies off the handle.

Spells

In a famous play by William Shakespeare, three witches make a spell to find out if Macbeth will become king. Here they are boiling up all sorts of horrible things…

ALL WITCHES: Double, double, toil and trouble;
  Fire burn, and cauldron bubble.
2nd WITCH: Fillet of a fenny snake,
  In the cauldron boil and bake;
  Eye of newt, and toe of frog,
  Wool of bat, and tongue of dog,
  Adder's fork, and blind-worm's sting,
  Lizard's leg, and owlet's wing—
ALL: Double, double, toil and trouble;
  Fire burn, and cauldron bubble.

Rhyme time

Witches love spells and brain teasers. See if you can work out these rhyming puzzles.

If a cat in a puddle = *a wet pet*

What is:

A witch on her own?   *a lone crone*

A plump puss?   *a fat cat*

A spell-maker's tickle?   *a witch itch*

Healing magic   *get well spell*

Here's another charm, written hundreds of years ago, which was supposed to get rid of bad habits:

Pick an apple and cut it in half sideways, so you can see the pips. Rub each half with the herb rosemary and say out loud the habit you want to get rid of. Perhaps: "I want to stop biting my nails!" Now wrap up the apple in a piece of white cloth (or tissue!) and bury it in the ground. As the apple rots away, so your bad habit will disappear… (At least, that is what the charm-writer thought.)

Toad in the Hole

What do witches love to eat? Toad in the hole! Here is a quick and simple recipe for a very yummy supper.

For The Toad:
8 good quality sausages
sunflower oil

For The Hole (or Batter!):
285ml/½ pint milk
115gr/4oz plain flour
a pinch of salt
3 eggs
1 adult to help with the oven

Method:
Get an adult to put on the oven to
220°C/425°F/Gas 7.

Mix together everything for the batter and put to one side.

Put 1cm of sunflower oil into the baking tin, then ask the adult to place this on the middle shelf of your oven.

When the oil is hot (after about 5 minutes), get the adult to add your sausages.

Wait for 15 minutes until the sausages have gone a nice brown colour.

At this point, ask the adult to take the tin out of the oven, and carefully pour your batter over the sausages. (The oil will be VERY HOT, so both of you should take care.)

Now the adult should gently put the tin back in the oven and close the door.

After 20 minutes, or when golden and crisp, ask the adult to remove your toad in the hole from the oven.

Eat as soon as it is cool enough.

YUM!

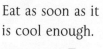

A Witchy Trick

See if you can fool your friends with this "magic" trick. Tell them you can see into the future. Set up a table and chair and put on a long black cape.

Ask your friends to call out the names of their favourite bands. Write the names down on pieces of paper, fold them and put them in a hat. (This is the trick: WRITE ONLY ONE NAME SEVERAL TIMES!)

In front of everyone, write on a separate piece of paper, which name you PREDICT will come out of the hat, but don't show what you have written. Fold the paper and give it to one of your friends. (You know which name will be chosen because there only IS one name...)

Get another friend to take a name
out of the hat and read it aloud.

Now get the first friend to open the piece
of paper where you wrote your
"prediction". And surprise, surprise, you guessed
the right name!

Quick! Get rid of all the other pieces of paper in the
hat before anyone can see how you did it!

Facts about Snowflakes

1 Every snowflake is made up of about 2-200 snow crystals. The snow crystal "grows" around a tiny microscopic speck of dust and whirls up and down inside a huge snow cloud. It is this movement which causes it to make the wonderful patterns we see.

2 Classic snow crystals have six sides, but you can find crystals that look like thin white hair!

3 The biggest snowflake ever recorded was 38cm across and 20cm thick.

4 The longest time anyone has managed to stay alive buried under the snow is believed to be 22 hours.

What goes cackle-cackle-cackle bonk?
A witch laughing her head off.

Do witches go on holiday?
Yes. They like to go away for a spell.

How do you make a witch scratch?
Take away her "w"

Have you spotted all of Theo's cat's pawprints?
There are 28. If you didn't get them all, go back
through these pages and look again!